The Tiger
Who Came to Tea

The Tiger Who Came to Tea

Written and illustrated by

Judith Kerr

HARPERCOLLINSPUBLISHERS

For Tacy and Matty

The Tiger Who Came to Tea
Copyright © 1968 by Judith Kerr
Manufactured in China
All rights reserved.
www.harperchildrens.com

Library of Congress Cataloging-in-Publication Data
Kerr, Judith.
  The tiger who came to tea / written and illustrated by Judith Kerr.
    p.   cm.
  Originally published: London : W. Collins, 1968.
  Summary: A tiger comes to tea at Sophie's house and eats and drinks everything in sight, so that there is
nothing left for Daddy's supper.
  ISBN 0-06-051780-8 — ISBN 0-06-051781-6 (lib. bdg.)
  [1. Tigers—Fiction.   2. Food—Fiction.]   I. Title.
PZ7.K46815 Ti   2002   [E]—dc21   2002024236   CIP   AC

Typography by Matt Adamec
1 2 3 4 5 6 7 8 9 10
❖
First published in Great Britain by William Collins Sons & Co. Ltd. in 1968

Once there was a little girl called Sophie,
and she was having tea with her mummy
in the kitchen.

Suddenly there was a ring at the door.

Sophie's mummy said,
"I wonder who that can be.

It can't be the milkman,
because he came this morning.

And it can't be the boy from the grocer,
because this isn't the day he comes.

And it can't be Daddy,
because he's got his key.

We'd better open the door
and see."

Sophie opened the door, and there was a big, furry, stripy tiger. The tiger said, "Excuse me, but I'm very hungry. Do you think I could have tea with you?" Sophie's mummy said, "Of course, come in."

So the tiger came into the kitchen and sat down at the table.

Sophie's mummy said, "Would you like a sandwich?"

But the tiger didn't take just one sandwich.

He took all the sandwiches on the plate

and swallowed them in one big mouthful. *Owp!*

And he still looked hungry,

so Sophie passed him the buns.

But again the tiger didn't eat just one bun.

He ate all the buns on the dish.

And then he ate all the biscuits

and all the cake,

until there was nothing

left to eat on the table.

So Sophie's mummy said,

"Would you like a drink?"

And the tiger drank

all the milk in the milk jug

and all the tea in the teapot.

And then he looked around the kitchen

to see what else he could find.

He ate all the supper

that was cooking in the saucepans . . .

. . . and all the food in the fridge,

and all the packets and tins in the cupboard . . .

and he drank all the milk,

and all the orange juice,

and all Daddy's beer,

and all the water in the tap.

Then he said,
"Thank you for my nice tea.
I think I'd better go now."
And he went.

Sophie's mummy said, "I don't know what to do.
I've got nothing for Daddy's supper, the tiger has
eaten it all."

And Sophie found she couldn't have her bath
because the tiger had drunk all the water in the tap.

Just then Sophie's daddy came home.

So Sophie and her mummy told him what had happened, and how the tiger had eaten all the food and drunk all the drink.

And Sophie's daddy said, "I know what we'll do.
I've got a very good idea. We'll put on our coats
and go to a café."

So they went out in the dark, and all the street lamps were lit, and all the cars had their lights on, and they walked down the road to a café.

And they had a lovely supper
with sausages and chips and ice cream.

In the morning
Sophie and her mummy
went shopping,
and they bought
lots more things to eat.

And they also bought
a very big tin of
Tiger Food,
in case the tiger should
come to tea again.

But he never did.